Helen Orme taught as a Special Needs Co-ordinator in a large comprehensive school. At the last count she had written around 40 books, many for reluctant readers.

Helen runs writing workshops for children and courses for teachers in both primary and secondary schools.

Boys!

Helen Orme

Boys!

by Helen Orme
Illustrated by Cathy Brett
Cover by Anna Torborg

Published by Ransom Publishing Ltd.
Rose Cottage, Howe Hill, Watlington, Oxon. OX49 5HB
www.ransom.co.uk

ISBN   978 184167 600 5

First published in 2007

Meet the Sisters ...

Siti and her friends are really close. So close she calls them her Sisters. They've been mates for ever, and most of the time they are closer than her real family.

Siti is the leader – the one who always knows what to do – but Kelly, Lu, Donna and Rachel have their own lives to lead as well.

Still, there's no one you can talk to, no one you can rely on, like your best mates. Right?

1

Wayne

Rachel's dad dropped her home late on Sunday evening.

"Mum," she called. "I'm home."

She went into the kitchen.

"Hi, I'm Wayne. You must be Rachel."

She blinked at him. He was a hunk.

"Yeah, Hi. Who, I mean what ..."

She was making a fool of herself she knew, but he was gorgeous.

At that moment Wil came down the stairs.

"Hi Rachel, this is …"

"Yeah, he said."

She turned away. "Better go and sort my stuff out."

"See you then," he said.

She went upstairs. Safe in her room, she stayed there until she heard the front door slam.

The door opened again. She listened – had they come back?

"Rachel." It was her mum. She went down. "Did you have a good weekend?"

"Yeah." She didn't talk too much about her weekends at her dad's. Mum always went a bit funny if she said too much.

"Who's that boy?"

"That new friend of Wil's? They've just moved in, down the road a bit. Wil met him at football. His name's Wayne."

"Yeah," thought Rachel. "I know."

2

He's a hunk

Next day she met up with her friends at school. She told them everything she'd found out about Wayne.

"He lives near us, he's eighteen, he's just finished at college and he's going to university next October."

"What's he look like?" asked Siti.

"He's a hunk," said Rachel.

"I can't wait to see him," said Donna.

"Hands off. I saw him first!"

Rachel and her friends called themselves the Sisters. They had known each other for years and were very close, just like real sisters.

The Sisters wanted to see Wayne, so did Rachel.

She kept asking Wil when Wayne would be round again.

"I dunno. When we meet up again, I suppose."

The Sisters started walking home with Rachel each day after school. When they met him they had to agree with Rachel. He was gorgeous.

One Saturday Rachel texted the Sisters.

"Wayne & Wil – city centre 10 o clock. B there."

"They're going to the computer store," she told them. "Then they're going to the match, but they're going to eat in the food hall before they go."

Siti looked at Rachel. "Like the gear," she said.

Rachel was really dressed up. She grinned. "He's never going to look at me in school uniform is he!"

3

All going wrong

They wandered around the shops for a while, but Rachel wanted to go and look for Wayne and Wil.

"Give it a rest," said Lu. "We can't go chasing him."

"Kelly always goes after Gary," said Rachel sulkily.

"That's different," said Siti. "He fancies her too, you know he does."

When they got to the food hall they couldn't see Wayne and Wil.

"What shall we eat?" asked Siti.

"Donna, over here!" They looked round. It was Donna's sister Marie, with her friend Susie. "Come and eat with us."

Rachel looked round. She still couldn't see Wayne.

"Why not?" she said. "But don't say anything about Wayne."

The Sisters went over and sat down.

"I'll get you all a drink," said Susie. "What do you want?"

Marie got her shopping out to show them the things she'd bought.

Suddenly they heard Wil's voice.

"Hi Marie. Hi kids."

Rachel glared at him. The Sisters weren't kids! Then she realised that Wayne was there too. She stopped glaring and smiled instead.

Susie came back.

"Hi guys, join us?" she said to Wil. She smiled at Wayne. "I'm Susie, this is Marie."

"Marie is Donna's sister," said Rachel. "Come and sit down."

She moved to make room, but Wil sat down next to her. Wayne sat between Donna and Susie.

Rachel was very, very cross. All her plans were going wrong!

4

In love

Rachel was in a mood.

Siti tried to make her feel better.

"After all, you did see him," she said. "That's the main thing."

"Yeah, but he didn't even look at me. He was too busy chatting up Susie."

"He talked to me," said Donna.

Rachel glared at her. "I'm fed up," she said. "I'm going home."

"Shall we come?" asked Siti.

"No, I'll be O.K. I'll talk later."

She headed off, back to the bus stop.

Siti looked at the others. "She's got it bad!"

"I don't blame her," said Donna. "I think he's dishy."

"He's O.K.," said Kelly, "But not my type."

Lu laughed. "Yeah, we all know your type."

"What are we gonna do about Rachel?" asked Lu. "She looked really miserable."

"We'd better go and catch her up," said Siti. "She'll still be at the bus stop."

Rachel was pleased when they caught up with her, and they decided to go to the cinema for the rest of the afternoon. By the time they went home she was feeling happier.

It was even better later that evening when Wil brought Wayne back to the house.

Wayne was really nice to her. He smiled a lot, talked about the match and asked about her friends.

She knew she was in love with him.

5

'I know
he likes me'

The trouble was, Donna was in love with him too. She wouldn't stop going on about him.

The others were fed up with Wayne. Every time either Rachel or Donna saw Wayne, or spoke to him, they kept on and on about it for ages.

"Even Kelly's not this bad about Gary," said Lu. "I'm fed up with hearing about Wayne."

"I think he's playing with them," said Siti. "He goes to Rachel's house to see Wil, but he's always chatting up Donna too."

Donna and Rachel were winding each other up. Donna went round to Rachel's when she thought Wayne might be there. Rachel was getting cross with her.

"It's not fair," she moaned to Siti. "She's not coming to see me. And she makes a real fool of herself when he comes round."

"I know he likes me," moaned Donna. "He always talks to me, not her. He's really interested in my riding. He said he'd like to come and watch."

In the end Rachel said she didn't want Donna going round to her house unless all the Sisters were going to be there.

Donna was very upset.

Siti, Kelly and Lu were upset too.

"I don't like this – they're getting worse," said Siti. "What can we do to sort things out?"

6

Talking to Donna

But even Siti couldn't sort things this time.

"At least they've stopped talking about Wayne all the time," said Kelly.

"But they won't talk to each other either," said Lu.

Siti tried to get the Sisters together to do things, but if Rachel said she would be there then Donna wouldn't come. If Donna went with them, Rachel said she had other things to do.

"Have you seen much of Wayne?" Siti asked Rachel.

Rachel burst into tears. "He's stopped coming round," she sobbed. "Wil goes out to meet him. I think it's because of Donna. She's spoilt everything!"

Siti tried to talk to Donna.

"I don't know why she blames me," she said. "It's her own fault."

She wouldn't talk about Wayne. "It's none of your business," she told Siti.

It wasn't like Donna. She usually told Siti everything. Donna didn't look happy, either.

Siti went round to Rachel's house after school to have a long talk with her.

"It's not worth splitting up the Sisters for a boy," she said.

"Yeah, you're right," agreed Rachel. "I've gone off him anyway. He's too big-headed for me."

"Come round to Donna's with me and we'll both talk to her."

But Rachel wouldn't.

"Not yet," she said. "You talk to her first. She might not want to make up."

Siti went on her own. Soon they would all be friends again. Everything was going to be all right.

She got to the corner. Outside Donna's door was Wayne! Siti stopped and watched. The door opened and Wayne went inside.

7

'I hate him!'

Siti was shocked. Now she would never get Rachel and Donna to be friends again. Even though Rachel said she didn't fancy Wayne any more, she would be really cross when she found out.

Next day at school Siti went to find Donna. She didn't know what she was going to say, but she had to say something.

She found Donna by herself in their empty form room. She was crying.

"Do you want to tell me?" asked Siti.

"I'm such an idiot! I've been pretending it was me he liked, but it's not. It's Marie!"

Siti patted her. "That explains everything," she thought.

"And now Rachel's not talking to me any more and you lot don't like me."

"Rachel's changed her mind," said Siti. "She doesn't like him any more."

"I hate him!" said Donna.

Siti waited until Donna stopped crying, then went off to find the others.

She told them about Marie.

"Poor Donna," said Rachel. "I know how she feels."

They went to find her.

Rachel rushed into the room and threw her arms round Donna.

"Boys!" she said. "They're just not worth it."

"By the way," said Lu. "Have you seen that new boy in year 10? I really fancy him."